THE

ICE DRAGON

✳ ✳ ✳ ❄ ✳ ✳ ✳

GEORGE R. R. MARTIN

Illustrated by

LUIS ROYO

TOR
TEEN

A TOM DOHERTY ASSOCIATES BOOK
NEW YORK

THE ICE DRAGON

Copyright © 1980 by George R. R. Martin

Illustrations copyright © 2014 by Luis Royo

Designed by Heather Saunders

A Tor Teen Book
Published by Tom Doherty Associates, LLC
175 Fifth Avenue
New York, NY 10010

www.tor-forge.com

Tor® is a registered trademark of Tom Doherty Associates, LLC.

The Library of Congress Cataloging-in-Publication Data
is available upon request.

ISBN 978-0-7653-7877-4 (hardcover)
ISBN 978-0-7653-7924-5 (e-book)

Tor Teen books may be purchased for educational, business, or promotional use. For information on bulk purchases, please contact Macmillan Corporate and Premium Sales Department at 1-800-221-7945, extension 5442, or write specialmarkets@macmillan.com.

Originally published by Ace Books in the volume *Dragons of Light*

First Edition: October 2006
First Tor Teen Edition: October 2014

Printed in the United States of America

0 9 8 7 6 5 4 3 2 1

THE

TO PHIPPS,

who thought of it first,

with all my love

CONTENTS

✳ ✳ ❊ ✳ ✳

THE

Chapter One

WINTER'S CHILD

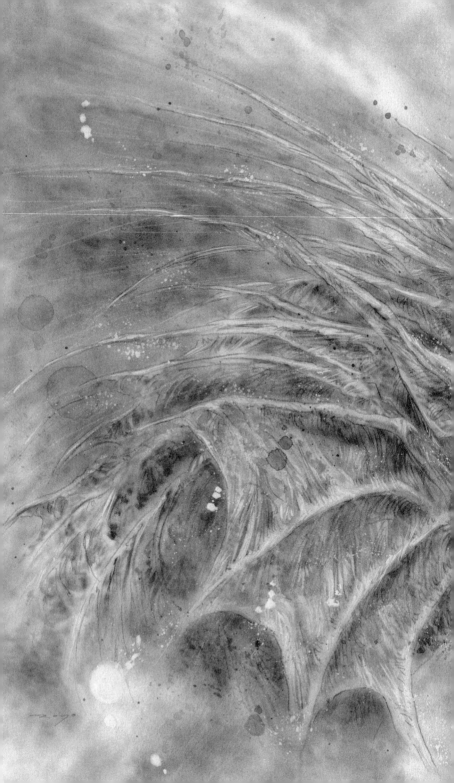

ADARA liked the winter best of all, for when the world grew cold the ice dragon came.

She was never quite sure whether it was the cold that brought the ice dragon or the ice dragon that brought the cold. That

was the sort of question that often troubled her brother Geoff, who was two years older than her and insatiably curious, but Adara did not care about such things. So long as the cold and the snow and the ice dragon all arrived on schedule, she was happy.

She always knew when they were due because of her birthday. Adara was a winter child, born during the worst freeze that anyone could remember, even Old Laura, who lived on the next farm and remembered things that had happened before anyone else was born.

People still talked about that freeze. Adara often heard them.

They talked about other things as well. They said it was the chill of that terrible freeze that had killed her mother, stealing in during her long night of labor past the great fire that Adara's father had built, and creeping under the layers of blankets that covered the birthing bed. And they said that the cold had entered Adara in the womb, that her skin had been pale blue and icy to the touch when she came forth, and that she had never warmed in all the years since. The winter had touched her, left its mark upon her, and made her its own.

It was true that Adara was always a child apart. She was a very serious little girl who seldom cared to play with the others. She was beautiful, people said, but in a strange, distant sort of way, with her pale skin and

blond hair and wide clear blue eyes. She smiled, but not often. No one had ever seen her cry. Once when she was five she had stepped upon a nail imbedded in a board that lay concealed beneath a snowbank, and it had gone clear through her foot, but Adara had not wept or screamed even then. She had pulled her foot loose and walked back to the house, leaving a trail of blood in the snow, and when she had gotten there she had said only, "Father, I hurt myself." The sulks and tempers and tears of ordinary childhood were not for her.

Even her family knew that Adara was different. Her father was a huge, gruff bear of a man who had little use for people in general, but a smile always broke across his face when Geoff pestered him with questions, and he was full of hugs and laughter for Teri, Adara's older sister, who was golden and freckled, and flirted shamelessly with all the local boys. Every so often he would hug Adara as well, but only during the long winters. But there would be no smiles then. He would only wrap his arms around her, and pull her small body tight against him with all his massive strength, sob deep in his chest, and fat wet tears would run down his ruddy cheeks. He never hugged her at all during the summers. During the summers he was too busy.

Everyone was busy during the summers except for Adara. Geoff would work with his father in the fields and ask endless questions about this and that, learning everything a farmer had to know. When he was not working he would run with his friends to the river, and have adventures. Teri ran the house and did the cooking, and worked a bit at the inn by the crossroads during the busy season. The innkeeper's daughter was her friend, and his youngest son was more than a friend, and she would always come back giggly and full of gossip and news from travelers and soldiers and king's messengers. For Teri and Geoff the summers were the best time, and both of them were too busy for Adara.

Their father was the busiest of all. A thousand things needed to be done each day, and he did them, and found a thousand more. He worked from dawn to dusk. His muscles grew hard and lean in summer, and he stank from sweat each night when he came in from the fields, but he always came in smiling. After supper he would sit with Geoff and tell him stories and answer his questions, or teach Teri things she did not know about cooking, or stroll down to the inn. He was a summer man, truly.

He never drank in summer, except for a cup of wine now and again to celebrate his brother's visits.

That was another reason why Teri and Geoff loved the summers, when the world was green and hot and bursting with life. It was only in summer that Uncle Hal, their father's younger brother, came to call. Hal was a dragonrider in service to the king, a tall slender

man with a face like a noble. Dragons cannot stand the cold, so when winter fell Hal and his wing would fly south. But each summer he returned, brilliant in the king's green-and-gold uniform, en route to the battle-grounds to the north and west of them. The war had been going on for all of Adara's life.

Whenever Hal came north, he would bring presents: toys from the king's city, crystal and gold jewelry, candies, and always a bottle of some expensive wine that he and his brother could share. He would grin at Teri and make her blush with his compliments, and entertain Geoff with tales of war and castles and dragons. As for Adara, he often tried to coax a smile out of her, with gifts and jests and hugs. He seldom succeeded.

For all his good nature, Adara did not like Hal; when Hal was there, it meant that winter was far away.

Besides, there had been a night when she was only four, and they thought her long asleep, that she overheard them talking over wine. "A solemn little thing," Hal said. "You ought to be kinder to her, John. You cannot blame *her* for what happened."

"Can't I?" her father replied, his voice thick with wine. "No, I suppose not. But it is hard. She looks like Beth, but she has none of Beth's warmth. The winter is in her, you know. Whenever I touch her I feel the chill, and I remember that it was for her that Beth had to die."

"You are cold to her. You do not love her as you do the others."

Adara remembered the way her father laughed then. "Love her? Ah, Hal. I loved her best of all, my little winter child. But she has never loved back. There is nothing in her for me, or you, any of us. She is such a cold little girl." And then he had begun to weep, even though it was summer and Hal was with him. In her bed, Adara listened and wished that Hal would fly away. She did not quite understand all that she had heard, not then, but she remembered it, and the understanding came later.

She did not cry; not at four, when she heard, or six, when she finally understood. Hal left a few days later, and Geoff and Teri waved to him excitedly when his wing passed overhead, thirty great dragons in proud formation against the summer sky. Adara watched with her small hands by her sides.

Chapter Two

❄ ❄ ❄ ❄ ❄

SECRETS IN THE SNOW

ADARA'S smiles were a secret store, and she spent of them only in winter. She could hardly wait for her birthday to come, and with it the cold. For in winter she was a special child.

She had known it since she was very little, playing with the others in the snow. The cold had never bothered her the way it did Geoff and Teri and their friends. Often Adara stayed outside alone for hours after the others had fled in search of warmth, or run off to Old Laura's to eat the hot vegetable soup she liked to make for the children. Adara would find a secret place in the far corner of the fields, a different place each winter, and there she would build a tall white castle, patting the snow in place with small bare bands, shaping it into towers and battlements like those Hal often talked about on the king's castle in the city. She would snap icicles off from the lower branches of trees, and use them for spires and spikes and guardposts, ranging them all about her castle. And often in the dead of winter would come a brief thaw and a sudden freeze, and overnight her snow castle would turn to ice, as hard and strong as she imagined real castles to be. All through the winters she would build on her castle, and no one ever knew. But always the spring would come, and a thaw not followed by a freeze; then all the ramparts and walls would melt away, and Adara would begin to count the days until her birthday came again.

Her winter castles were seldom empty. At the first frost each year, the ice lizards would come wriggling out of their burrows, and the fields would be overrun with the tiny blue creatures, darting this way and that, hardly seeming to touch the snow as they skimmed across it. All the children played with the ice lizards. But the others were clumsy and cruel, and they would snap the fragile little animals in two, breaking them between their fingers as they might break an icicle hanging from a roof. Even Geoff, who was too kind ever to do something like that, sometimes grew curious, and held the lizards too long in his efforts to examine them, and the heat of his hands would make them melt and burn and finally die.

Adara's hands were cool and gentle, and she could hold the lizards as long as she liked without harming them, which always made Geoff pout and ask angry questions. Sometimes she would lie in the cold, damp snow and let the lizards crawl all over her, delighting in the light touch of their feet as they skittered across her face. Sometimes she would wear ice lizards hidden in her hair as she went about her chores, though she took care never to take them inside where the heat of the fires would kill them. Always she would gather up scraps after the family ate, and bring them to the secret place where her castle was a-building, and there she would scatter them. So the castles she erected were full of kings and courtiers every winter; small furry creatures that snuck out from the woods, winter birds with pale white plumage, and hundreds and hundreds

of squirming, struggling ice lizards, cold and quick and fat. Adara liked the ice lizards better than any of the pets the family had kept over the years.

But it was the ice dragon that she loved.

She did not know when she had first seen it. It seemed to her that it had always been a part of her life, a vision glimpsed during the deep of winter, sweeping across the frigid sky on wings serene and blue. Ice dragons were rare, even in those days, and whenever it was seen the children would all point and wonder, while the old folks muttered and shook their heads. It was a sign of a long and bitter winter when ice dragons were abroad in the land. An ice dragon had been seen flying across the face of the moon on the night Adara had been born, people said, and each winter since it had been seen again, and those winters had been very bad indeed, the spring coming later each year. So the people would set fires and pray and hope to keep the ice dragon away, and Adara would fill with fear.

But it never worked. Every year the ice dragon returned. Adara knew it came for her.

The ice dragon was large, half again the size of the scaled green war dragons that Hal and his fellows flew. Adara had heard legends of wild dragons larger than mountains, but she had never seen any. Hal's dragon was big enough, to be sure, five times the size of a horse, but it was small compared to the ice dragon, and ugly besides.

The ice dragon was a crystalline white, that shade of white that is so hard and cold that it is almost blue. It was covered with hoarfrost, so when it moved its skin broke and crackled as the crust on the snow crackles beneath a man's boots, and flakes of rime fell off.

Its eyes were clear and deep and icy.

Its wings were vast and batlike, colored all a faint translucent blue. Adara could see the clouds through them, and oftentimes the moon and stars, when the beast wheeled in frozen circles through the skies.

Its teeth were icicles, a triple row of them, jagged spears of unequal length, white against its deep blue maw.

When the ice dragon beat its wings, the cold winds blew and the snow swirled and scurried and the world seemed to shrink and shiver. Sometimes when a door flew open in the cold of winter, driven by a sudden gust of wind, the householder would run to bolt it and say, "An ice dragon flies nearby."

And when the ice dragon opened its great mouth, and exhaled, it was not fire that came streaming out, the burning sulfurous stink of lesser dragons.

The ice dragon breathed cold.

Ice formed when it breathed. Warmth fled. Fires

guttered and went out, shriven by the chill. Trees froze through to their slow secret souls, and their limbs turned brittle and cracked from their own weight. Animals turned blue and whimpered and died, their eyes bulging and their skin covered over with frost.

The ice dragon breathed death into the world; death and quiet and cold. But Adara was not afraid. She was a winter child, and the ice dragon was her secret.

She had seen it in the sky a thousand times. When she was four, she saw it on the ground.

She was out building on her snow castle, and it came and landed close to her, in the emptiness of the snow-covered fields. All the ice lizards ran away.

Adara simply stood. The ice dragon looked at her for ten long heartbeats before it took to the air again. The wind shrieked around her and through her as it beat its wings to rise, but Adara felt strangely exulted.

Later that winter it returned, and Adara touched it. Its skin was very cold. She took off her glove nonetheless. It would not be right otherwise. She was half afraid it would burn and melt at her touch, but it did not. It was much more sensitive to heat than even the ice lizards, Adara knew somehow. But she was special, the winter child, cool. She stroked it, and finally gave its wing a kiss that hurt her lips. That was the winter of her fourth birthday, the year she touched the ice dragon.

Chapter Three

❄ ❄ ❄ ❄ ❄

THE
RISING
COLD

THE winter of her fifth birthday was the year she rode upon it for the first time.

It found her again, working on a different castle at a different place in the fields, alone as ever. She watched it come, and ran to it when it landed, and pressed herself against it. That had been the summer when she heard her father talking to Hal.

They stood together for long minutes until finally Adara, remembering Hal, reached out and tugged at the dragon's wing with a small hand. And the dragon beat its great wings once, and then extended them flat against the snow, and Adara scrambled up to wrap her arms about its cold white neck.

Together, for the first time, they flew.

She had no harness or whip, as the king's dragon-riders use. At times the beating of the wings threatened to shake her loose from where she clung, and the coldness of the dragon's flesh crept through her clothing and bit and numbed her child's flesh. But Adara was not afraid.

They flew over her father's farm, and she saw Geoff

looking very small below, startled and afraid, and knew he could not see her. It made her laugh an icy, tinkling laugh, a laugh as bright and crisp as the winter air.

They flew over the crossroads inn, where crowds of people came out to watch them pass.

They flew above the forest, all white and green and silent.

They flew high into the sky, so high that Adara could not even see the ground below, and she thought she glimpsed another ice dragon, way off in the distance, but it was not half so grand as *hers*.

They flew for most of the day, and finally the dragon swept around in a great circle and spiraled down, gliding on its stiff and glittering wings. It let her off in the field where it had found her, just after dusk.

Her father found her there, and wept to see her, and hugged her savagely. Adara did not understand that, nor why he beat her after he had gotten her back to the house. But when she and Geoff had been put to sleep,

she heard him slide out of his own bed and come padding over to hers. "You missed it all," he said. "There was an ice dragon, and it scared everybody. Father was afraid it had eaten you."

Adara smiled to herself in the darkness, but said nothing.

She flew on the ice dragon four more times that winter, and every winter after that. Each year she flew further and more often than the year before, and the ice dragon was seen more frequently in the skies above their farm.

Each winter was longer and colder than the one before.

Each year the thaw came later.

And sometimes there were patches of land, where the ice dragon had lain to rest, that never seemed to thaw properly at all.

There was much talk in the village during her sixth

year, and a message was sent to the king. No answer ever came.

"A bad business, ice dragons," Hal said that summer when he visited the farm. "They're not like real dragons, you know. You can't break them or train them. We have tales of those that tried, found frozen with their whip and harness in hand. I've heard about people that have lost hands or fingers just by touching one of them. Frostbite. Yes, a bad business."

"Then why doesn't the king do something?" her father demanded. "We sent a message. Unless we can kill the beast or drive it away, in a year or two we won't have any planting season at all."

Hal smiled grimly. "The king has other concerns. The war is going badly, you know. They advance every summer, and they have twice as many dragonriders as we do. I tell you, John, it's bad up there. Some year I'm not going to come back. The king can hardly spare men to go chasing an ice dragon." He laughed. "Besides, I don't think anybody's ever killed one of the things. Maybe we should just let the enemy take this whole province. Then it'll be *his* ice dragon."

But it wouldn't be, Adara thought as she listened. No matter what king ruled the land, it would always be *her* ice dragon.

Chapter Four

✳ ✳ ✳ ✳ ✳

FIRES
IN THE
NORTH

HAL departed and summer waxed and waned. Adara counted the days until her birthday. Hal passed through

again before the first chill, taking his ugly dragon south for the winter. His wing seemed smaller when it came flying over the forest that fall, though, and his visit was briefer than usual, and ended with a loud quarrel between him and her father.

"They won't move during the winter," Hal said. "The winter terrain is too treacherous, and they won't risk an advance without dragonriders to cover them from above. But come spring, we aren't going to be able to hold them. The king may not even try. Sell the farm now, while you can still get a good price. You can buy another piece of land in the south.

"This is my land," her father said. "I was born here. You too, though you seem to have forgotten it. Our parents are buried here. And Beth too. I want to lie beside her when I go."

"You'll go a lot sooner than you'd like if you don't listen to me," Hal said angrily. "Don't be stupid, John. I know what the land means to you, but it isn't worth your life." He went on and on, but her father would not be moved. They ended the evening swearing at each other, and Hal left in the dead of night, slamming the door behind him as he went.

Adara, listening, had made a decision. It did not matter what her father did or did not do. She would stay. If she moved, the ice dragon would not know where to find her when winter came, and if she went too far south it would never be able to come to her at all.

It did come to her, though, just after her seventh birthday. That winter was the coldest one of all. She flew so often and so far that she scarcely had time to work on her ice castle.

Hal came again in the spring. There were only a dozen dragons in his wing, and he brought no presents that year. He and her father argued once again. Hal raged and pleaded and threatened, but her father was stone. Finally Hal left, off to the battlefields.

That was the year the king's line broke, up north near some town with a long name that Adara could not pronounce.

Teri heard about it first. She returned from the inn one night flushed and excited. "A messenger came through, on his way to the king," she told them. "The enemy won some big battle, and he's to ask for reinforcements. He said our army is retreating."

Their father frowned, and worry lines creased his brow. "Did he say anything of the king's dragonriders?" Arguments or no, Hal was family.

"I asked," Teri said. "He said the dragonriders are the rear guard. They're supposed to raid and burn, delay the enemy while our army pulls back safely. Oh, I hope Uncle Hal is safe!"

"Hal will show them," Geoff said. "Him and Brimstone will burn 'em all up."

Their father smiled. "Hal could always take care of himself. At any rate, there is nothing we can do. Teri, if any more messengers come through, ask them how it goes."

She nodded, her concern not quite covering her excitement. It was all quite thrilling.

In the weeks that followed, the thrill wore off as the people of the area began to comprehend the magnitude of the disaster. The king's highway grew busier and busier, and all the traffic flowed from north to south, and all the travelers wore green and gold. At first the soldiers marched in disciplined columns, led by officers wearing golden helmets, but even then they were less than stirring. The columns marched wearily, and the uniforms were filthy and torn, and the swords and pikes and

axes the soldiers carried were nicked and ofttimes stained. Some men had lost their weapons; they limped along blindly, empty-handed.

And the trains of wounded that followed the columns were often longer than the columns themselves. Adara stood in the grass by the side of the road and watched them pass. She saw a man with no eyes supporting a man with only one leg, as the two of them walked together. She saw men with no legs, or no arms, or both. She saw a man with his head split open by an axe, and many men covered with caked blood and filth, men who moaned low in their throats as they walked. She *smelled* men with bodies that were horribly greenish and puffed up. One of them died and was left abandoned by the side of the road. Adara told her father, and he and some of the men from the village came out and buried him.

Most of all, Adara saw the burned men. There were dozens of them in every column that passed, men whose skin was black and seared and falling off, who had lost an arm or a leg or half of a face to the hot breath of a dragon. Teri told them what the officers said, when they stopped at the inn to drink or rest: the enemy had many, many dragons.

Chapter Five

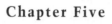

ASHES

**F**OR almost a month the columns flowed past, more every day. Even Old Laura admitted that she had never seen so much

traffic on the road. From time to time a lone messenger on horseback rode against the tide, galloping towards the north, but always alone.

After a time everyone knew there would be no reinforcements.

An officer in one of the last columns advised the people of the area to pack up whatever they could carry and move south. "They are coming," he warned. A few listened to him, and indeed for a week the road was full of refugees from towns further north. Some of them told frightful stories. When they left, more of the local people went with them.

But most stayed. They were people like her father, and the land was in their blood.

The last organized force to come down the road was a ragged troop of cavalry, men as gaunt as skeletons riding horses with skin pulled tight around their ribs. They thundered past in the night, their mounts heaving and foaming, and the only one to pause was a pale young officer, who reined his mount up briefly and shouted, "Go, go. They are burning everything!" Then he was off after his men.

The few soldiers who came after were alone or in small groups. They did not always use the road, and they did not pay for the things they took.

Then no one came at all. The road was deserted.

The innkeeper claimed he could smell ashes when the wind blew from the north. He packed up his family and went south. Teri was distraught. Geoff was wide-eyed and anxious and only a bit frightened. He asked a thousand questions about the enemy, and practiced at being a warrior. Their father went about his labors, busy as ever. War or no war, he had crops in the field. He smiled less than usual, however, and he began to drink, and Adara often saw him glancing up at the sky while he worked.

Adara wandered the fields alone, played by herself in the damp summer heat, and tried to think of where she would hide if her father tried to take them away.

Last of all, the king's dragonriders came, and with them Hal.

There were only four of them. Adara saw the first one, and went and told her father, and he put his hand on her shoulder and together they watched it pass, a solitary green dragon with a vaguely tattered look. It did not pause for them.

Two days later, three dragons flying together came into view, and one of them detached itself from the others and circled down to their farm while the other two headed south.

Uncle Hal was thin and grim and sallow-looking. His dragon looked sick. Its eyes ran, and one of its wings had been partially burned, so it flew in an awkward, heavy manner, with much difficulty. "Now will you go?" Hal said to his brother, in front of all the children.

"No. Nothing has changed."

Hal swore. "They will be here within three days," he said. "Their dragonriders may be here even sooner."

"Father, I'm scared," Teri said.

He looked at her, saw her fear, hesitated, and finally turned back to his brother. "I am staying. But if you would, I would have you take the children."

Now it was Hal's turn to pause. He thought for a moment, and finally shook his head. "I can't, John. I would, willingly, joyfully, if it were possible. But it isn't. Brimstone is wounded. He can barely carry me. If I took on any extra weight, we might never make it."

Teri began to weep.

"I'm sorry, love," Hal said to her. "Truly I am." His fists clenched helplessly.

"Teri is almost full-grown," their father said. "If her weight is too much, then take one of the others."

Brother looked at brother, with despair in their eyes. Hal trembled. "Adara," he said finally. "She's small and light." He forced a laugh. "She hardly weighs anything at all. I'll take Adara. The rest of you take horses, or a wagon, or go on foot. But go you must."

"We will see," their father said non-committally. "You take Adara, and keep her safe for us."

"Yes," Hal agreed. He turned and smiled at her. "Come, child. Uncle Hal is going to take you for a ride on Brimstone."

Adara looked at him very seriously. "No," she said. She turned and slipped through the door and began to run.

They came after her, of course, Hal and her father and even Geoff. But her father wasted time standing in the door, shouting at her to come back, and when he began to run he was ponderous and clumsy, while Adara was indeed small and

light and fleet of foot. Hal and Geoff

stayed with her longer, but Hal was weak, and Geoff

soon winded himself, though he sprinted hard at her

heels for a few moments. By the time Adara reached

the nearest wheat field, the three of them were well

behind her. She quickly lost herself amid the grain,

and they searched for hours in vain while she made her way carefully towards the woods.

When dusk fell, they brought out lanterns and torches and continued their search. From time to time she heard her father swearing, or Hal calling out her name. She stayed high in the branches of the oak she had climbed, and smiled down at their lights as they combed back and forth through the fields. Finally she drifted off to sleep, dreaming about the coming of winter and wondering how she would live until her birthday. It was still a long time away.

Chapter Six

❋ ❋ ❋ ❋ ❋

FLEEING
THE FIRE

AWN woke her; dawn and a noise in the sky.

Adara yawned and blinked, and heard it again. She shinnied to the uppermost limb

of the tree, as high as it would bear her, and pushed aside the leaves.

There were dragons in the sky.

She had never seen beasts quite like these. Their scales were dark and sooty, not green like the dragon Hal rode. One was a rust color and one was the shade of dried blood and one was black as coal. All of them had eyes like glowing embers, and steam rose from their nostrils, and their tails flicked back and forth as their dark, leathery wings beat the air. The rust-colored one opened its mouth and roared, and the forest shook to its challenge, and even the branch that held Adara trembled just a little. The black one made a noise too, and when it opened its maw a spear of flame lanced out, all orange and blue, and touched

the trees below. Leaves withered and blackened, and smoke began to rise from where the dragon's breath had fallen. The one the color of blood flew close overhead, its wings creaking and straining, its mouth half-open. Between its yellowed teeth Adara saw soot and cinders, and the wind stirred by its passage was fire and sandpaper, raw and chafing against her skin. She cringed.

On the backs of the dragons rode men with whip and lance, in uniforms of black and orange, their faces hidden behind dark helmets. The one on the rust dragon gestured with his lance, pointing at the farm buildings across the fields. Adara looked.

Hal came up to meet them.

His green dragon was as large as their own, but somehow it seemed small to Adara as she watched it climb upwards from the farm. With its wings fully extended, it was plain to see how badly injured it was;

the right wing tip was charred, and it leaned heavily to one side as it flew. On its back, Hal looked like one of the tiny toy soldiers he had brought them as a present years before.

The enemy dragonriders split up and came at him from three sides. Hal saw what they were doing. He tried to turn, to throw himself at the black dragon head-on, and flee the other two. His whip flailed angrily, desperately. His green dragon opened its mouth, and roared a challenge, but its flame was pale and short and did not reach the enemy.

The others held their fire. Then, on a signal, their dragons all breathed as one. Hal was wreathed in flames.

His dragon made a high wailing noise, and Adara saw that it was burning, *he* was burning, they were all burning, beast and master both. They fell heavily to the ground, and lay smoking amidst her father's wheat.

The air was full of ashes.

Adara craned her head around in the other direction, and saw a column of smoke rising from beyond the forest and the river. That was the farm where Old Laura lived with her grandchildren and *their* children.

When she looked back, the three dark dragons were circling lower and lower above her own farm. One by one they landed. She watched the first of the riders dismount and saunter towards their door.

She was frightened and confused and only seven, after all. And the heavy air of summer was a weight upon her, and it filled her with a helplessness and thickened all her fears. So Adara did the only thing she knew, without thinking, a thing that came naturally to her. She climbed down from her tree and ran. She ran across the fields and through the woods, away from the farm and her family and the dragons, away from all of it. She ran until her legs throbbed with pain, down in the direction of the river. She ran to the coldest place she knew, to the deep caves underneath the river bluffs, to chill shelter and darkness and safety.

And there in the cold she hid. Adara was a winter child, and cold did not bother her. But still, as she hid, she trembled.

Day turned into night. Adara did not leave her cave.

She tried to sleep, but her dreams were full of burning dragons.

She made herself very small as she lay in the darkness, and tried to count how many days remained until her birthday. The caves were nicely cool; Adara could almost imagine that it was not summer after all, that it was winter, or near to winter. Soon her ice dragon would come for her, and she would ride on its back to the land of always-winter, where great ice castles and cathedrals of snow stood eternally in endless fields of white, and the stillness and silence were all.

It almost felt like winter as she lay there. The cave

grew colder and colder, it seemed. It made her feel safe. She napped briefly. When she woke, it was colder still. A white coating of frost covered the cave walls, and she was sitting on a bed of ice. Adara jumped to her feet and looked up towards the mouth of the cave, filled with a wan dawn light. A cold wind caressed her. But it was coming from outside, from the world of summer, not from the depths of the cave at all.

She gave a small shout of joy and climbed and scrambled up the ice-covered rocks.

Outside, the ice dragon was waiting for her.

It had breathed upon the water, and now the river was frozen, or at least a part of it was, although one could see that the ice was fast melting as the summer sun rose. It had breathed upon the green grass that grew along the banks, grass as high as Adara, and now the tall blades were white and brittle, and when the ice dragon moved its wings the grass cracked in half and tumbled, sheared as clean as if it had been cut down with a scythe.

The dragon's icy eyes met Adara's, and she ran to it and up its wing, and threw her arms about it. She knew she had to hurry. The ice dragon looked smaller than she had ever seen it, and she understood what the heat of summer was doing to it.

"Hurry, dragon," she whispered. "Take me away, take me to the land of always-winter. We'll never come back here, never. I'll build you the best castle of all, and take care of you, and ride you every day. Just take me away, dragon, take me home with you."

The ice dragon heard and understood. Its wide translucent wings unfolded and beat the air, and bitter arctic winds howled through the fields of summer. They rose. Away from the cave. Away from the river. Above the forest. Up and up. The ice dragon swung around to the north. Adara caught a glimpse of her father's farm, but it was very small and growing smaller. They turned their back to it, and soared.

Then a sound came to Adara's ears. An impossible sound, a sound that was too small and too far away for her to ever have heard it, especially above the beating of the ice dragon's wings. But she heard it nonetheless. She heard her father scream.

Hot tears ran down her cheeks, and where they fell upon the ice dragon's back they burned small pockmarks in the frost. Suddenly the cold beneath her hands was biting, and when she pulled one hand away Adara saw the mark that it had made upon the dragon's neck. She was scared, but still she clung. "Turn back," she whispered. "Oh, *please*, dragon. Take me back."

She could not see the ice dragon's eyes, but she knew what they would look like. Its mouth opened and a blue-white plume issued, a long cold streamer that hung in the air. It made no noise; ice dragons are silent. But in her mind Adara heard the wild keening of its grief.

"Please," she whispered once again. "Help me." Her voice was thin and small.

The ice dragon turned.

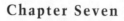

Chapter Seven

❋ ❋ ❋ ❋ ❋

COLD
FURY

THE three dark dragons
were outside of the

barn when Adara returned,
feasting on the burned and
blackened carcasses
of her father's

stock. One of the dragonriders was standing near them, leaning on his lance and prodding his dragon from time to time.

He looked up when the cold gust of wind came shrieking across the fields, and shouted something, and sprinted for the black dragon. The beast tore a last hunk of meat from her father's horse, swallowed, and rose reluctantly into the air. The rider flailed his whip.

Adara saw the door of the farmhouse burst open. The other two riders rushed out, and ran for their dragons.

The black dragon roared, and its fire came blazing up at them. Adara felt the searing of heat, and a shudder went through the ice dragon as the flames played along its belly. Then it craned its long neck around, and fixed its baleful empty eyes upon the enemy, and opened its frost-rimmed jaws. Out from among its icy teeth its breath came streaming, and that breath was pale and cold.

It touched the left wing of the coal-black dragon beneath them, and the dark beast gave a shrill cry of pain, and when it beat its wings again, the frost-covered wing broke in two. Dragon and dragonrider began to fall.

The ice dragon breathed again.

They were frozen and dead before they hit the ground.

The rust-colored dragon was flying at them, and the dragon the color of blood with its bare-chested rider. Adara's ears were filled with their angry roaring, and she could feel their hot breath around her, and see the air shimmering with heat, and smell the stink of sulfur.

Two long swords of fire crossed in midair, but nei-

ther touched the ice dragon, though it shriveled in the heat, and water flew from it like rain whenever it beat its wings.

The blood-colored dragon flew too close, and the breath of the ice dragon blasted the rider. His bare chest turned blue before Adara's eyes, and moisture condensed on him in an instant, covering him with frost. He screamed, and died, and fell from his mount, though his harness remained behind, frozen to the neck of his dragon. The ice dragon closed on it, wings screaming the secret song of winter, and a blast of flame met a blast of cold. The ice dragon shuddered once again, and twisted away, dripping. The other dragon died.

But the last dragonrider was behind them now, the enemy in full armor on the dragon whose scales were the brown of rust. Adara screamed, and even as she did the fire enveloped the ice dragon's wing. It was gone in less than an instant, but the wing was gone with it, melted, destroyed.

The ice dragon's remaining wing beat wildly to slow its plunge, but it came to earth with an awful crash. Its legs shattered beneath it, and its wing snapped in two places, and the impact of the landing threw Adara from its back. She tumbled to the soft earth of the field, and rolled, and struggled up, bruised but whole.

The ice dragon seemed very small now, very broken. Its long neck sank wearily to the ground, and its head rested amid the wheat.

The enemy dragonrider came swooping in, roaring with triumph. The dragon's eyes burned. The man flourished his lance and shouted.

The ice dragon painfully raised its head once more, and made the only sound that Adara ever heard it make: a terrible thin cry full of melancholy, like the sound the north wind makes when it moves around the towers and battlements of the white castle that stands empty in the land of always-winter.

When the cry had faded, the ice dragon sent cold into the world one final time: a long smoking blue-white stream of cold that was full of snow and stillness and the end of all living things. The dragonrider flew right into it, still brandishing whip and lance. Adara watched him crash.

Then she was running, away from the fields, back to the house and her family within, running as fast as she could, running and panting and crying all the while like a seven-year-old.

Adara did not know what to do, but she found Teri, whose tears had dried by then, and they freed Geoff, and then untied their father. Teri nursed him, and cleaned out his wounds. When his eyes opened and he saw Adara he smiled. She hugged him very hard, and cried for him.

By night he said he was fit enough to travel. They

crept away under cover of darkness, and took the king's road south.

Her family asked no questions then, in those hours of darkness and fear. But later, when they were safe in the south, there were questions endlessly. Adara gave them the best answers she could. But none of them ever believed her, except for Geoff, and he grew out of it when he got older. She was only seven, after all, and she did not understand that ice dragons are never seen in summer, and cannot be tamed nor ridden.

Besides, when they left the house that night, there was no ice dragon to be seen. Only the huge dark corpses of three war dragons and the smaller bodies of three dragonriders in black and orange. And a pond that had never been there before, a small quiet pool where the water was very cold. They had walked around it carefully, headed towards the road.

Chapter Eight

❋ ❋ ❋ ❋ ❋

SPRING

THEIR father worked for another farmer for three years in the south. He saved whatever he could, and he seemed happy. "Hal is gone, and my land," he would tell Adara, "and I am sad for that. But it is all right. I have my daughter back." For the winter was gone from her now, and she smiled and laughed and even wept like other little girls.

Three years after they had fled, the king's
army routed the enemy in a great battle, and
the king's dragons burned the foreign capital. In the
peace that followed, the northern provinces changed

hands once more. Teri had recaptured her spirit and married a young trader, and she remained in the south. Geoff and Adara returned with their father to the farm.

When the first frost came, all the ice lizards came out, just as they had always done. Adara watched them with a smile on her face, remembering the way it had been. But she did not try to touch them. They were cold and fragile little things, and the warmth of her hands would hurt them.

ABOUT THE AUTHOR

✵ ✵ ✵ ✵ ✵

Author of the *New York Times* bestselling A Song of Ice and Fire series that begins with *A Game of Thrones,* called "the American Tolkien" by *Time* magazine, GEORGE R. R. MARTIN is one of the leading authors of fantasy today.

ABOUT THE ILLUSTRATOR

❄ ❄ ❄ ❄ ❄

LUIS ROYO is a prolific Spanish artist best known for his lush fantasy illustrations. Over thirty books of his collected art have been published, including *Women, Dead Moon, Visions,* and the Malefic Times series. Royo's artwork was featured in *Spectrum 3* and has been exhibited in Barcelona, Madrid, Milan, New York, Seattle, and St. Petersburg. Visit him online at www.luisroyo.com.